# Bat Count

## A Citizen Science Story

by Anna Forrester
illustrated by Susan Detwiler

The sun is dropping behind the ridge and the red-winged blackbirds have quit their squalling, so I know it's almost time.

Mom and Dad wash dishes while I gather twigs. When my hands are full, I carry them down to the fire pit and pile them into a little teepee.

I'm allowed to build fires on my own. "You know the way, Jojo," Mom says, "just keep an eye on our baby boys!"

The "baby boys" are my twin brothers, Jakie and Lou. They are three, but Mom still calls them babies. After I was born, it took a long time for any more babies to come. When Mom found out she was having twins, she called it "double luck." I'd never seen her so happy.

The twins are digging for worms. They don't remember the counts. We started the bat counts after the twins were born.

When I was little, Mom used to sweep bat droppings from the barn once a week. She sprinkled them in her garden, and swore they made her plants grow bigger.

Once, before the twins came, Mom and I spotted a mama bat hanging upside down in the hayloft, wedged into a gap between two boards. She hugged her baby tight with her wings. Both bats were small like mice—not scary at all. They looked a little fragile, really.

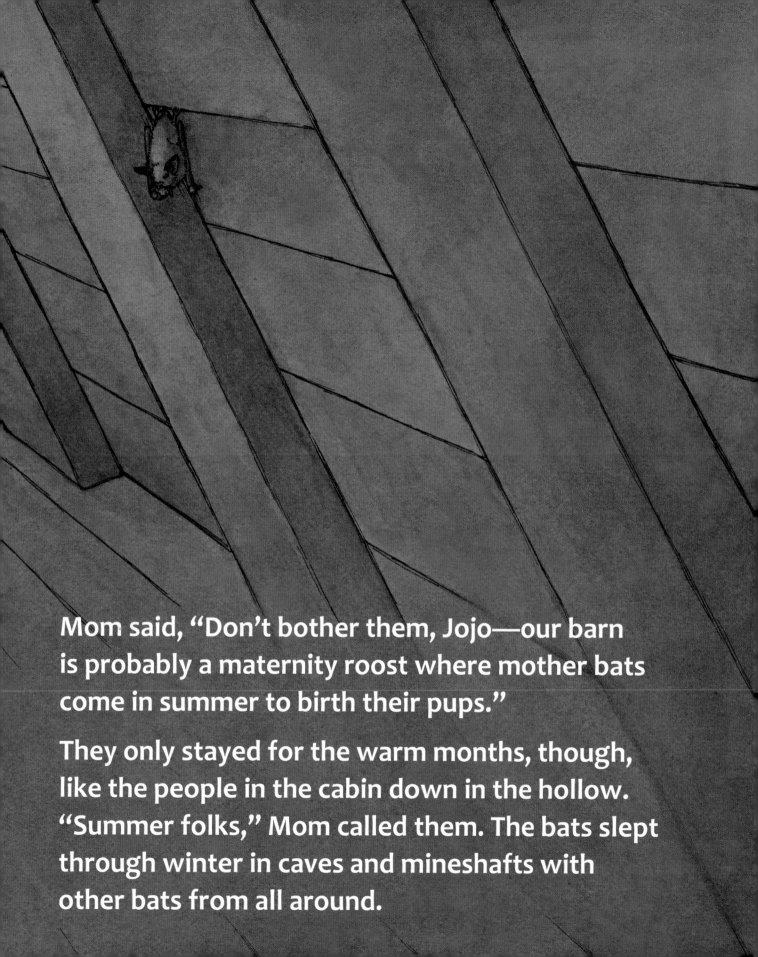

Mom said, "Don't bother them, Jojo—our barn is probably a maternity roost where mother bats come in summer to birth their pups."

They only stayed for the warm months, though, like the people in the cabin down in the hollow. "Summer folks," Mom called them. The bats slept through winter in caves and mineshafts with other bats from all around.

The year the twins came, there were fewer droppings. Mom was busy juggling double bottles and double diapers and didn't give it much thought. Back then, Mom only had time for the baby boys.

The year after, there were even fewer, and she started worrying. The newspaper told how thousands of bats were dying in their winter caves because of a disease called white-nose syndrome. But there's hope that some won't catch the disease—or can maybe recover from it.

The bat scientists began tracking them. They asked people to do counts when the bats fly out at night to feed, and to fill out forms and send their numbers in.

That year we began our counts. The most we counted was thirty-nine bats.

The summer after that, we counted again and there were just ten.

And this year when the bats first arrived in June, it wasn't much of a count at all: there was only one single bat.

We didn't sweep up droppings once this whole summer.

Mom said bats have one pup at a time—like people—just once a year. By mid-summer the pups, if there are any, will fly out alongside their mothers. So now, in August, we count again. If our barn really is a maternity roost, and our bat has pupped, we'll have two. And maybe the bats can recover.

I strike a match and touch it to my twig teepee. The pile catches quickly, and smoke puffs up.

The screen door slams, and Mom and Dad start down the driveway.

Jakie and Lou drop their shovels and dash to meet them. While they ride piggyback down to the fire, I lay three logs over top of the flames.

We lie down on our backs in the grass in a neat row: me, then Mom, then Jakie, then Lou, then Dad.

The bats usually fly out from a gap at the top of the barn on the side facing the pond. That's where we watch.

We haven't been lying in the grass for more than five minutes when a bat—the bat, our bat—shoots out. My heart jumps, and Mom squeezes my hand.

Dad says in a hushed voice, "Jojo, keep watching by the roof. I'll keep an eye on the sides so we know if she goes back in."

Mom and I snuggle up close and lie still.

We wait and wait. I wonder that the twins aren't more squirmy and then, over the crickets, I hear slow, deep breathing. They are asleep.

Dad whispers, "Our bat has flown back into the barn, through a hole at the corner."

We wait and watch.

Mom sighs. "Well, there is still one!"

The way she says it, I know that she thinks the count is done. "Five more minutes, Mom, please!" I whisper.

"Okay," she whispers back. "But then it's time to take these baby boys in to bed."

I hold my breath and cross my fingers.

Finally, Mom nudges me. "Okay," she says, "it's time." I let out all my breath in a big sigh. And just at that moment I see them. One, two, three small shadows, fluttering out from the barn. Three!

"Mom!" I shout-whisper. "Did you see?"

She squeezes my hand. "I did!"

"There were three, Mom, three!"

Dad shakes his head and smiles. "Wow!"

We lie by the fire a while longer, snuggled up, before agreeing that the count is done. Mom and Dad each heave a baby boy up onto a shoulder and we start back up to the house.

"Mom, you were right," I whisper. "Our barn is a maternity roost. And there were three. That mama had twins!"

"She sure did," Mom nods.

"She must be so happy!" I say. "Maybe next year all three will come back and they will have more babies, and the same thing the year after that, and the year after that, and by the time the twins are big the barn will be full up again with bats."

Mom puts her free arm around me. "I hope so," she says. "Though I think that mama bat would be just as happy if she had one baby all by itself." And she hugs me.

I hold the screen door open for everyone. And when I look back, I can just make out three tiny shadows zig-zagging over the pond.

# For Creative Minds

## Bat Facts

Bats are a type of mammal. Like other mammals, bats are vertebrate animals (have a spine or spinal column), they breathe oxygen from the air, they are warm-blooded, they have fur or hair, most give birth to live young, and their young drink milk from their mothers. But bats are a special type of mammal: they are the only mammal that can fly.

There are 1,200 to 1,300 different species of bats. Bats make up about 20% of all the mammals in the world. There are two main types of bats.

**Megabats** are also called fruit bats. They live in warm, tropical climates, and usually roost in trees. They use their large eyes to find food in the dark. Megabats usually eat fruit or drink nectar from plants.

**Microbats** are usually smaller than megabats. They use their ears to find food. They make a high-pitched squeak as they fly. This sound bounces off objects and the bats listen to the echo to learn about their surroundings. This is called **echolocation**. Microbats live in warm and cold climates all around the world. They roost in caves, crevices, buildings, and trees. Many microbats eat insects (insectivores). They can also eat fruit, nectar, blood, and fish.

Many people think that bats are blind. Have you ever heard the phrase, "blind as a bat"? But bats can actually see very well. They just can't see color. But that doesn't slow them down at all. Since bats are active at night (nocturnal), they don't miss seeing a lot of color.

There are 40 to 50 different species of bats in the United States. Before the bats were affected by white-nose syndrome, little brown bats were the most common bat in the United States. A little brown bat eats half its body-weight in insects every night!

Most bats, like humans, have one pup at a time. But, also like humans, they can sometimes have more.

# Bat Bodies

Match the body part to its location on this little brown bat. Do you have any body parts similar to a bat's? Does a bat have any body parts that you do not?

The **forearm** is the part of the arm between the elbow and where the fingers begin.

The **elbow** is a joint. It connects the forearm with the upper arm.

Bats use their **ears** to listen.

The bony **tail** helps support the wing membrane.

Bats use their **feet** to grip things. They have five toes on each foot.

Bats use their **nose** to smell and to breathe. Some bats use their nose to echolocate!

The **shoulder** is a joint. It connects the arm with the rest of the body.

Bats have a claw on each **thumb**. They use their thumbs to climb, crawl, or fight.

Bats have a thin layer of skin (membrane) that stretches between their long fingers, arms, and legs. Bats use these **wings** to fly.

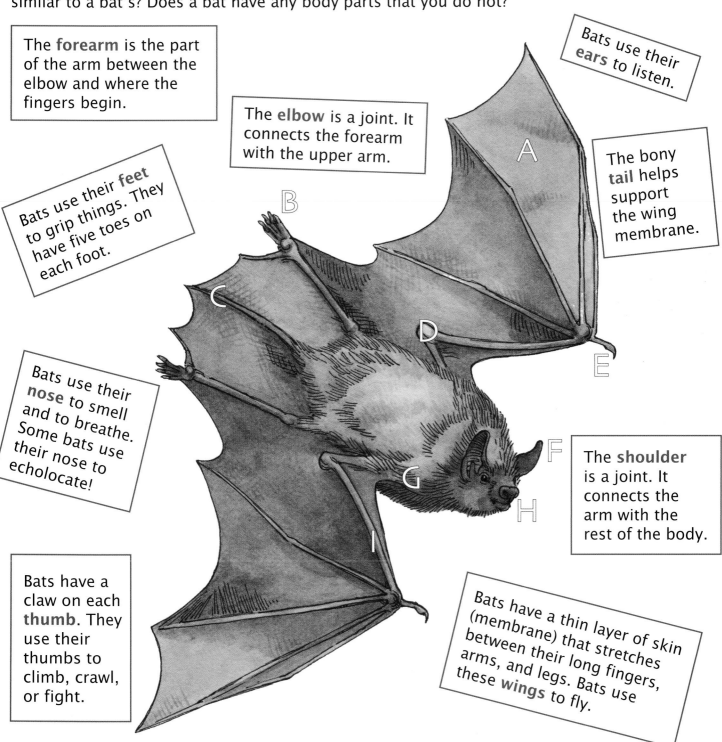

Answers: A-wings, B-feet, C-tail, D-elbow, E-thumb, F-ear, G-shoulder, H-nose, I-forearm

# White-Nose Syndrome

Healthy bat

Bat with WNS

White-nose syndrome, or WNS, is a disease that affects hibernating bats. It is caused by a fungus that grows in cold, wet environments like caves, mineshafts, and rock crevices. Many bats hibernate in these places through the winter. The fungus grows on bats' noses, wings, and ears.

Bats squeeze together to stay warm when they hibernate. If one bat is sick with WNS, the fungus can spread to other bats hibernating in the same space.

When bats have WNS, they act strangely. They wake up and move around a lot, even when they should be sleeping. They move closer to the entrance of the cave or mineshaft. Sometimes bats with WNS even fly out into the cold, winter air.

Hibernating bats usually sleep through the winter. When they wake up and move around, they burn through the body fat that they had stored. This body fat was supposed to sustain them through the winter. There is nothing for the bats to eat until spring, so their bodies grow weak. This makes the bats vulnerable to other kinds of sickness as well.

When WNS is introduced to a place where bats are hibernating, it can kill as many as 90-100% of the bats. WNS has killed millions of bats since it was first discovered in New York in 2006. Since then, WNS has spread across eastern and central United States and Canada, and even to the west coast in Washington State.

## You can help bats!

- Build a bat house. Look up directions online or at your library. Your bat house will provide a safe place for bats to roost or have pups in the summer.

- Participate in a Bat Count. Help scientists track the bat population in your area.

- Do not explore caves or mines where bats are hibernating. If you see bats hibernating, leave them alone.

- If you see a bat in the wild, do not try to touch it. If the bat looks sick or injured, contact a local wildlife rescue organization. Wild animals don't know that you are trying to help them, and can be dangerous if they are scared. If a bat accidentally touches you, tell your doctor.

Bats affected by WNS in 2016

# Citizen Science

Scientists are studying WNS, but they cannot do it all alone. They rely on **citizen scientists** to help. Citizen scientists, like Jojo and her family, are volunteers who make observations and gather data. They can help professional scientists in their research. There are many different projects, all around the world and online, where citizen scientists can help with research. *Would you like to be a citizen scientist?*

Bat counts, like other citizen science activities, are carefully planned by the scientists conducting the research. These scientists need to make sure that the data they get is usable and reliable. Often the scientists create simple forms or worksheets for citizen scientists to fill in. This makes sure that the scientists get all the information they need about the bats and where they were counted.

Many different organizations participate in bat counts. If you want to get involved in a bat count, contact your local Department of Natural Resources, Fish and Wildlife Department, Game Commission, nature center, or bat conservation organization. They can tell you more about the bats in your area and train you to participate in bat counts.

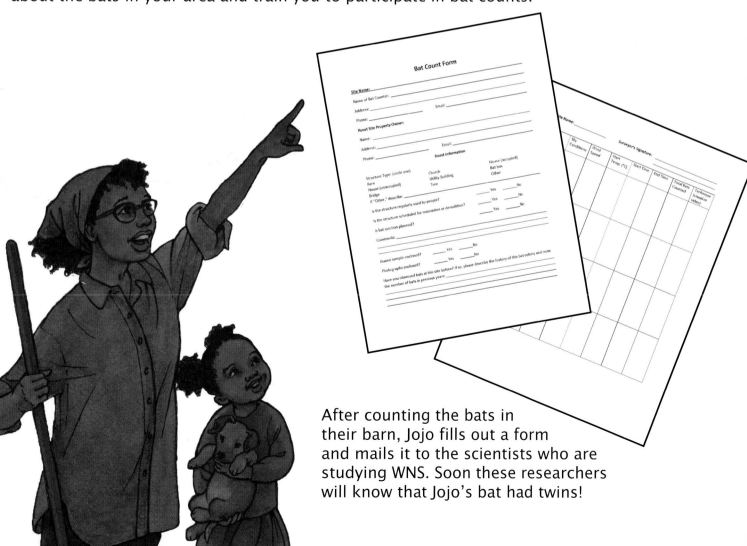

After counting the bats in their barn, Jojo fills out a form and mails it to the scientists who are studying WNS. Soon these researchers will know that Jojo's bat had twins!

To Mira, Adrie, Mitch . . . and our bats.—AF

For Felix, with love.—SD

The author donates a portion of her royalties to Bat Conservation International.

Thanks to Katie Gillies, Director of the Imperiled Species Program at Bat Conservation International (www.batcon.org), and Catherine J. Hibbard, White-nose Syndrome Communications Leader with the U.S. Fish and Wildlife Service, for verifying the accuracy of the information in this book.

Library of Congress Cataloging-in-Publication Data

Names: Forrester, Anna, 1966- | Detwiler, Susan, illustrator. | Bat
    Conservation International.
Title: Bat count : a citizen science story / by Anna Forrester ; illustrated
    by Susan Detwiler.
Description: Mt. Pleasant, SC : Arbordale Publishing, 2016. | Audience: Age
    4-8. | Audience: K to grade 3. | "Bat Conservation International." |
    Includes bibliographical references.
Identifiers: LCCN 2016043587 (print) | LCCN 2016044993 (ebook) | ISBN
    9781628558944 (english hardcover) | ISBN 9781628558951 (english pbk.) |
    ISBN 9781628558968 (spanish pbk.) | ISBN 9781628558975 (English
    Downloadable eBook) | ISBN 9781628558999 (English Interactive
    Dual-Language eBook) | ISBN 9781628558982 ( Spanish Downloadable eBook) |
    ISBN 9781628559002 (Spanish Interactive Dual-Language eBook)
Subjects: LCSH: Bats--Juvenile literature. | Bats--Counting--Juvenile
    literature. | Bats--Losses--Juvenile literature.
Classification: LCC QL737.C5 F67 2016 (print) | LCC QL737.C5 (ebook) | DDC
    599.4--dc23
LC record available at https://lccn.loc.gov/2016043587

Translated into Spanish: ***Contando los murciélagos: Una historia de ciencias cívicas***

Lexile® Level: AD 730

key phrases: bats, citizen science, conservation, disease, families, migration/hibernation, outside activity, white-nose syndrome

Bibliography:
*Bat Conservation International.* N.p., n.d. Web. 08 Sept. 2016.
Burns, Loree Griffin., and Ellen Harasimowicz. *Citizen Scientists: Be a Part of Scientific Discovery from
    Your Own Backyard.* New York: H. Holt, 2012. Print.
Landgraf, Greg. *Citizen Science Guide for Families: Taking Part in Real Science.* N.p.: Huron Street,
    2013. Print.
*White Nose Syndrome.* N.p., n.d. Web. 08 Sept. 2016.

Manufactured in China, December 2016
This product conforms to CPSIA 2008
First Printing

Arbordale Publishing
Mt. Pleasant, SC 29464
www.ArbordalePublishing.com